WOOF meow tweet-tweet

Cécile Boyer

Seven Footer Kids

Do you know how to tell the difference
between a dog, a cat and a bird?

The dog lives outside during the day.
He protects the house.

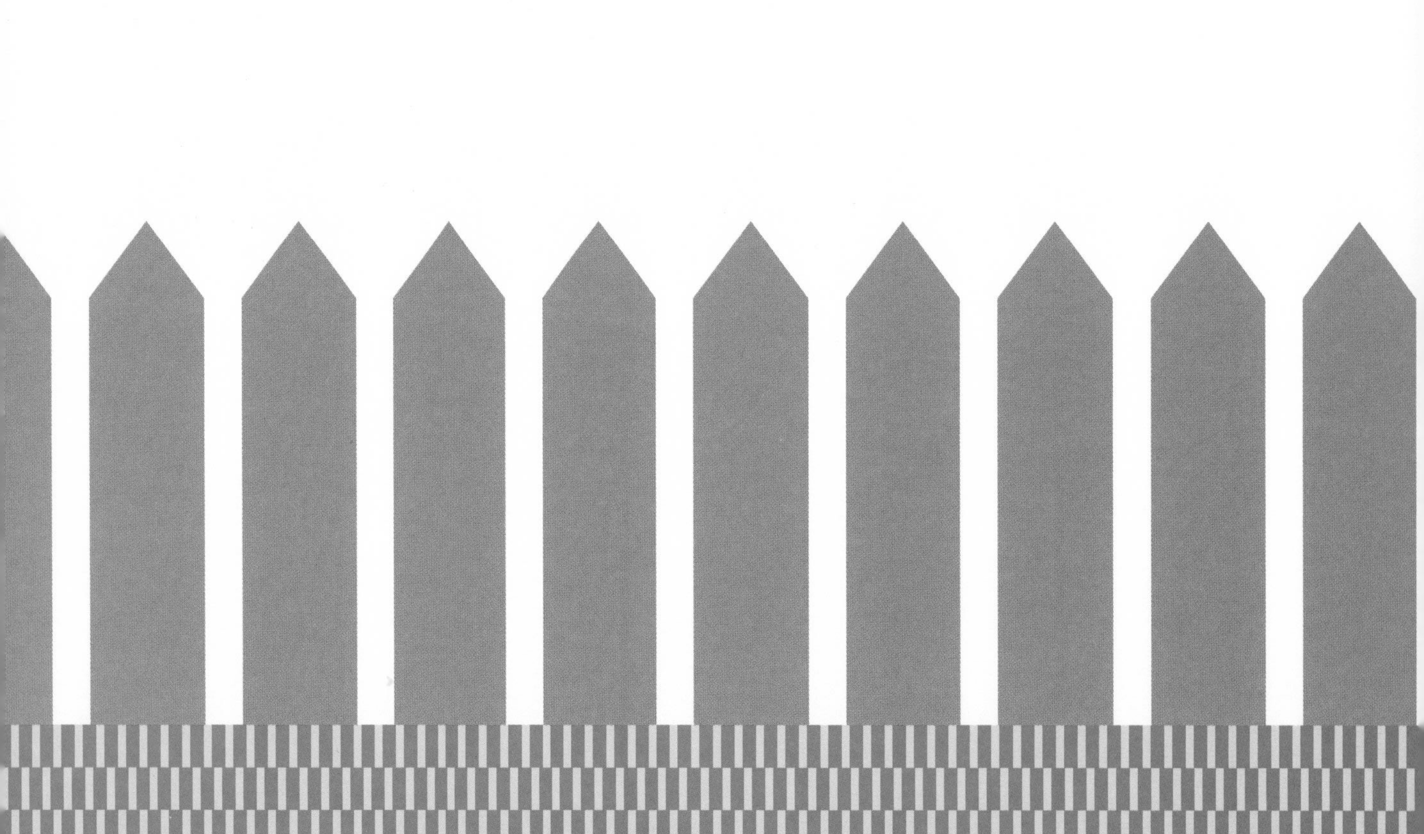

The cat prefers the comfort
of a nice interior.

meow

The bird does not like his cage.

tweet-tweet

Because he is meant to fly high,
high in the sky.

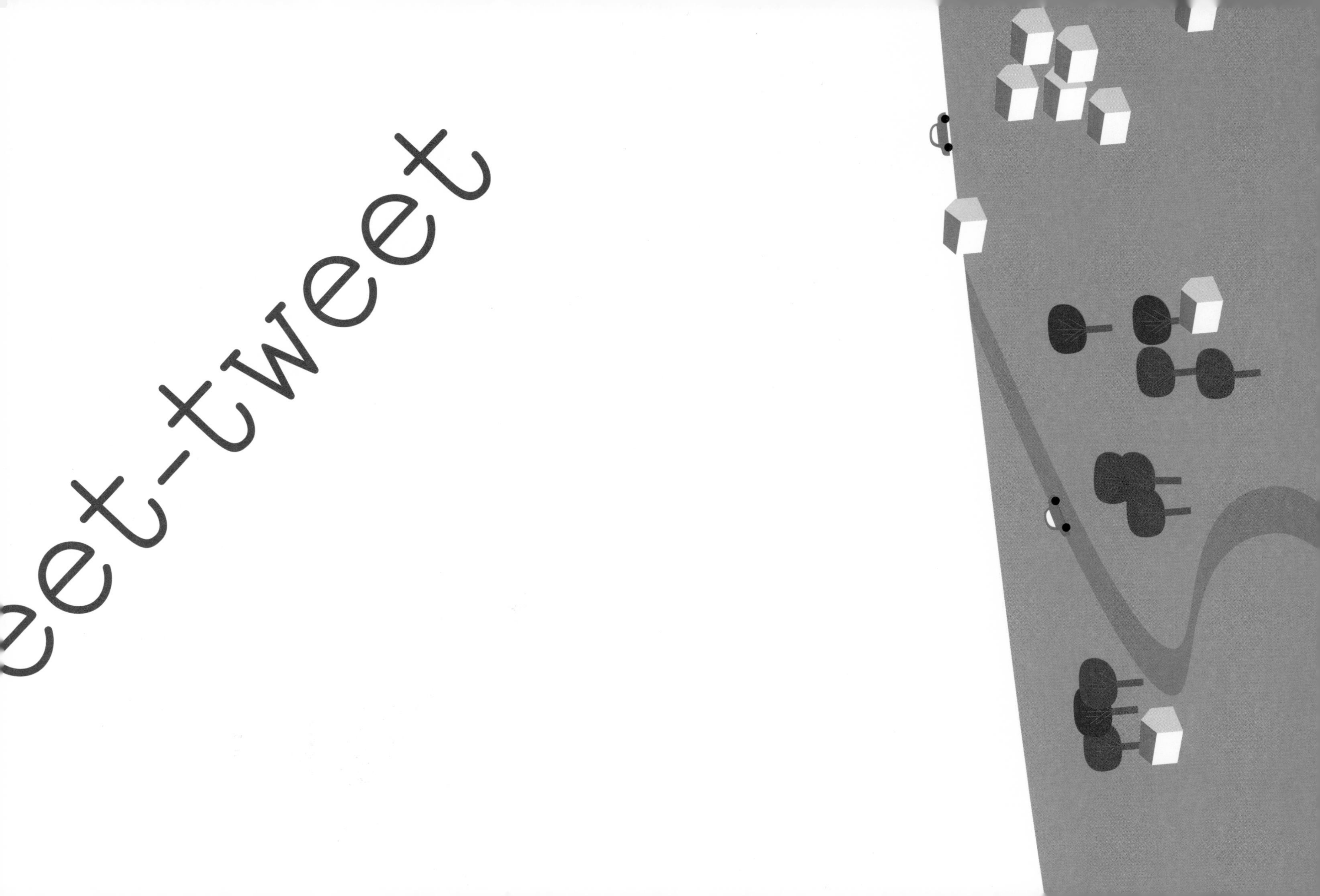
eet-tweet

The cat is a solitary creature.
At night, he walks alone on the rooftops.

meow

The dog needs company
and he's eager to please his master.
"Beg!"
"Sit!"
WOOF
WOOF

"Lie down!"

"Good dog! You're a very good dog!"

tweet-tweet

The bird, perched on a branch,
sings a happy song.

The cat loves to venture onto the table
near fragile objects.

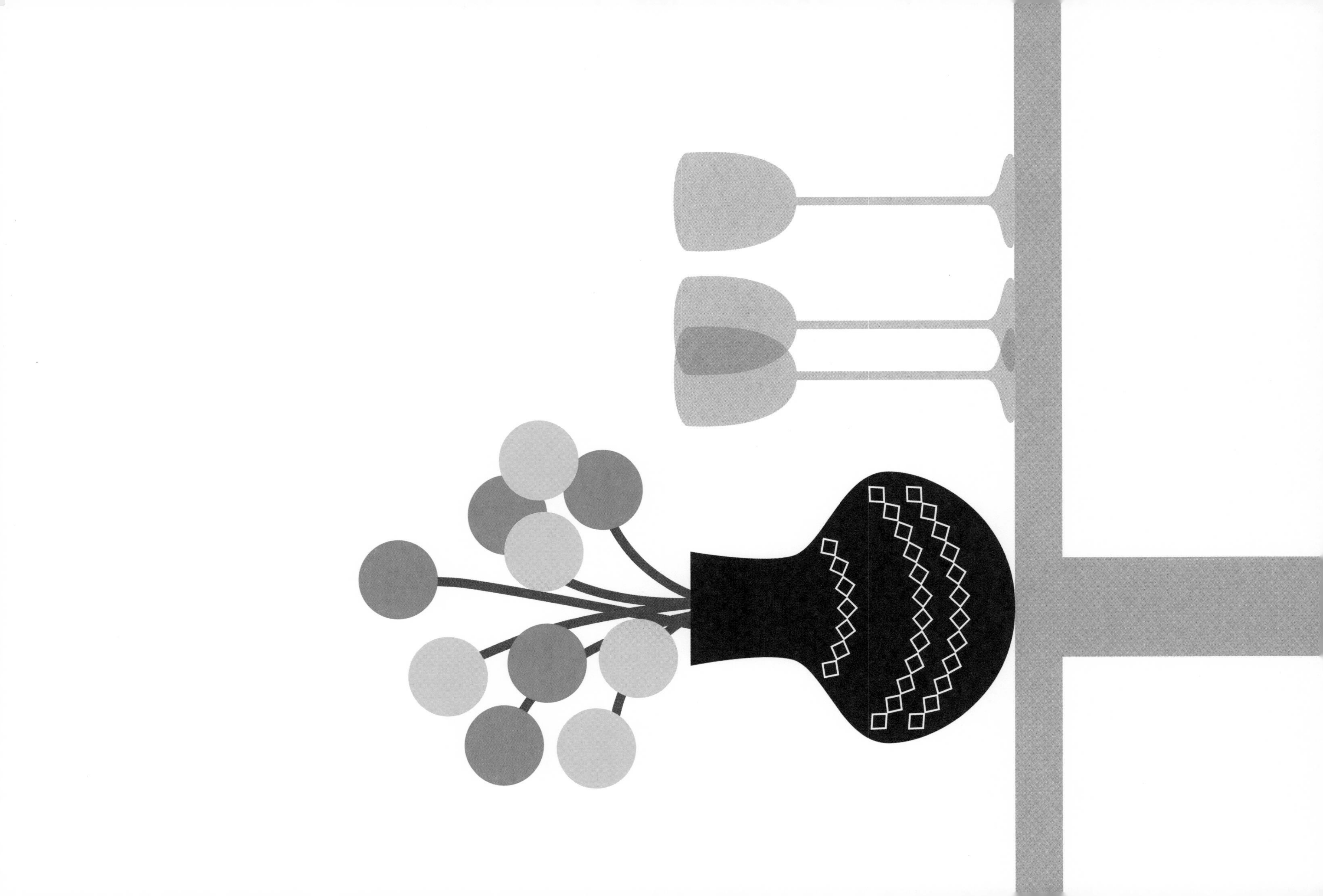

Fortunately nothing gets broken
because cats are very careful.

A dog might have to pee on a wall.
He just can’t help himself.

WOOF

tweet-tweet

The bird can make a mess, too.
Watch out when one flies over you!

More than anything,
the dog loves to chase a ball.

WOOF

WOOF

WOOF

WOOF
WOOF
WOOF

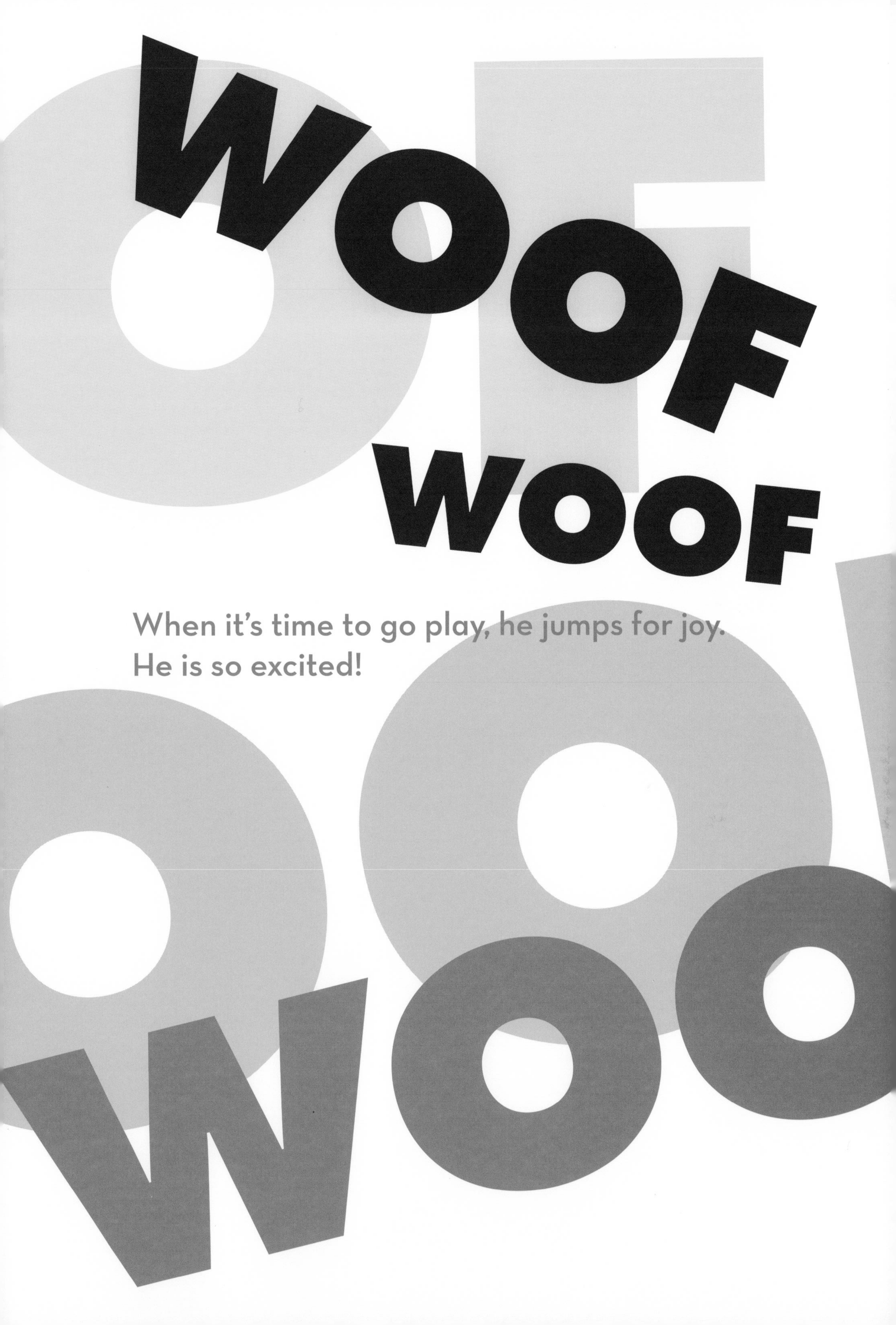

When it’s time to go play, he jumps for joy.
He is so excited!

During all this commotion, the cat
goes to sleep on the couch.

meow

tweet-tweet
tweet-tweet
tweet-tweet
tweet-tweet
tweet-tweet
tweet-tweet
tweet-tweet
tweet-tweet

And the bird is safe on high,
surrounded by others of his kind.

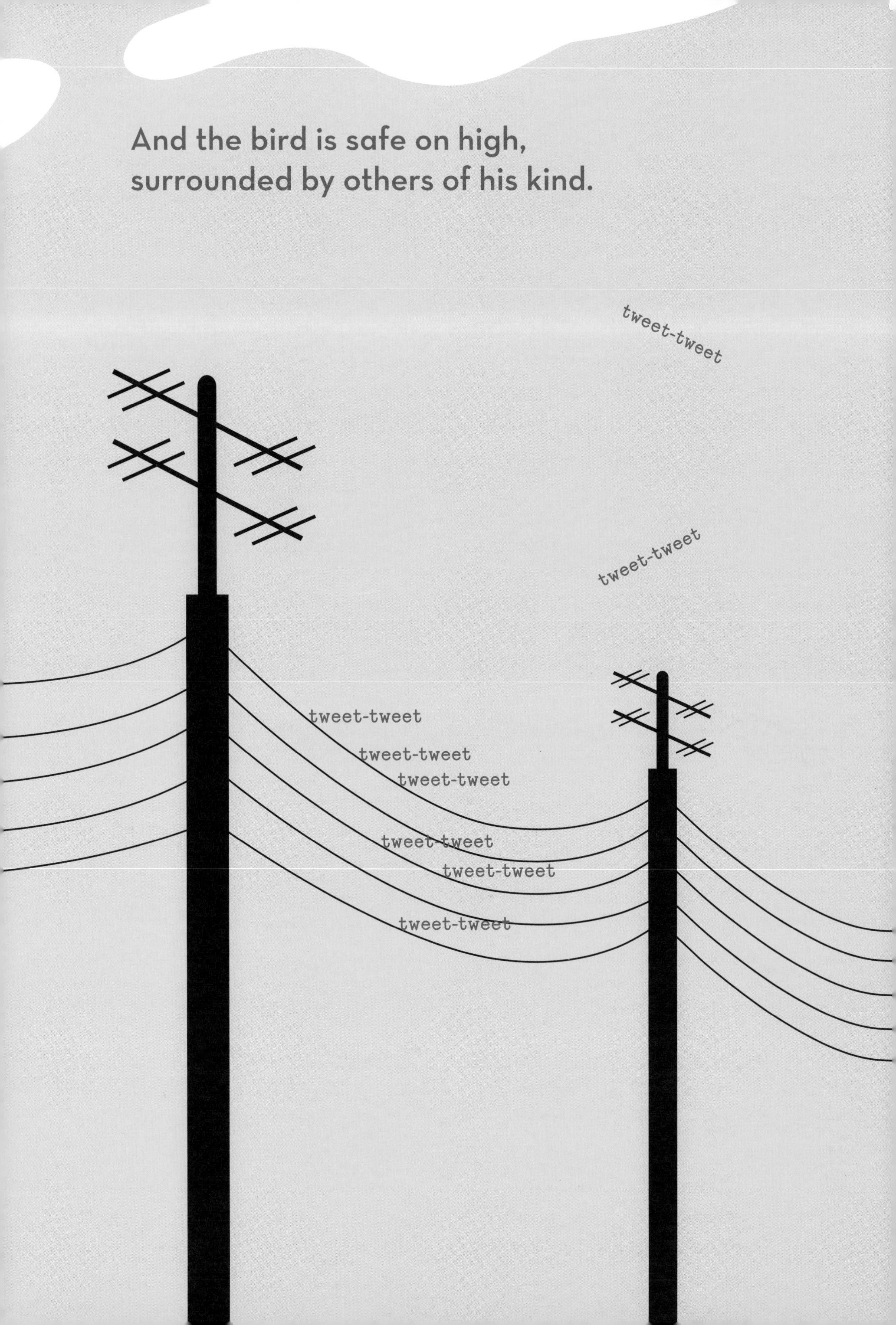

Sometimes dogs, cats and birds will cross paths. Do you know what happens then?

When a dog encounters a bird,
not much occurs.
WO

tweet-tweet
OF

But if the dog and the cat meet,
there is always a fight!

Terrified, the cat runs up a tree.
meow

But the bird was there first,
quietly sitting on a branch.

tweet-tweet

In less than a second, the cat pounces!

meow
WOOF

tweet-tweet

Luckily the bird flies off in time.

Each can go back to his own business.

All three still have many days to live
as a dog, a cat and a bird.

This book was written and illustrated
by Cécile Boyer.

was set in the font Futura, designed
by Paul Renner.

meow
was set in a font specially designed
for this book by Emmanuel Pevny.

tweet-tweet
was set in the font Elementa,
designed by Mindaugas Strockis.

The text was set in Neutraface,
a font designed by Christian
Schwartz, based on lettering
by Richard Neutra.

This book was manufactured
in Shen Zhen, Guang Dong,
P.R China, in December 2010
by Print Plus, Ltd.

First published in France as
Ouaf Miaou Cui-Cui

Published by Seven Footer Kids,
an imprint of Seven Footer Press,
a division of Seven Footer
Entertainment, LLC, New York

ISBN-13: 978-1-934734-60-5
10 9 8 7 6 5 4 3 2 1